Disney • PIXAR

THE WORLD OF

Disney • PIXAR

"I'm faster than fast. Quicker than quick. I am Lightning!" says Lightning
McQueen during his first Piston Cup race.

In the lead is The King, followed by top competitor Chick Hicks. Suddenly
Chick slams into another car, causing a wreck to try to block McQueen.

The other cars head to their pits for repairs. But McQueen ignores his
pit crew and stays in the race to take the lead. Near the finish line,
his tires pop. The King and Chick catch up—and the race ends in a
three-way tie!

A tie-breaker race will be held in California. McQueen wants to get there quickly. He tells his trailer driver, Mack, to drive all night on the Interstate.

"I'll stay up with you!" McQueen promises. But he breaks his promise and nods off.

Soon Mack falls asleep too. Then he swerves, causing McQueen to roll out of the trailer and onto the highway. Cars speed towards him!

McQueen exits the Interstate to try to find Mack but ends up speeding along Old Highway 66. A local sheriff chases McQueen. So McQueen speeds up—and wrecks the main road in a small town called Radiator Springs.

A friendly tow truck named Mater tows McQueen to the Radiator Springs Courthouse. All the cars from the town are there. Doc Hudson is the town judge.  He wants to kick McQueen out of town for ruining the main road. But Sally, the town attorney, disagrees.

"Come on, make this guy fix the road," Sally says. "We are a town worth fixing."

Mater hooks McQueen up to Bessie, the town's road-paver.

"How long is this going to take?" McQueen asks.

"If you do it right, about five days," Doc replies.

McQueen is in a hurry to get to California, so he works fast repairing the road with Bessie. After just one hour, he declares that he is finished.

Mater is the first to drive on the road. It's covered with bumps and potholes.

"It looks awful," says Sally.

"Scrape it off. Start over again," Doc orders McQueen.

"Hey, I'm not a bulldozer, I'm a racecar," McQueen protests.

At that, Doc challenges McQueen to a race. If McQueen wins, he can leave town. If Doc wins, McQueen must stay and fix the road the right way.

McQueen is sure he will win. But to his surprise, Doc leaves him in the dust. McQueen ends up in a ditch! Trusty Mater gives McQueen a tow.

McQueen goes back to fix the road.  That night, Mater takes McQueen out for some fun. Mater drives up to some sleeping tractors and honks his horn.  The tractors tip over!

Driving back to town, Mater asks, "What's so important about this race of yours anyway?"

"I'll be the first rookie to win," says McQueen. "When I do, we're talking a big new sponsor with private helicopters."

"You think one day I can get a ride in one of them helicopters?" asks Mater.

"Yeah, sure," McQueen replies.

"I knew it. I made a good choice in my best friend," Mater says.

HIGHWAY 66 ROAD TRIP

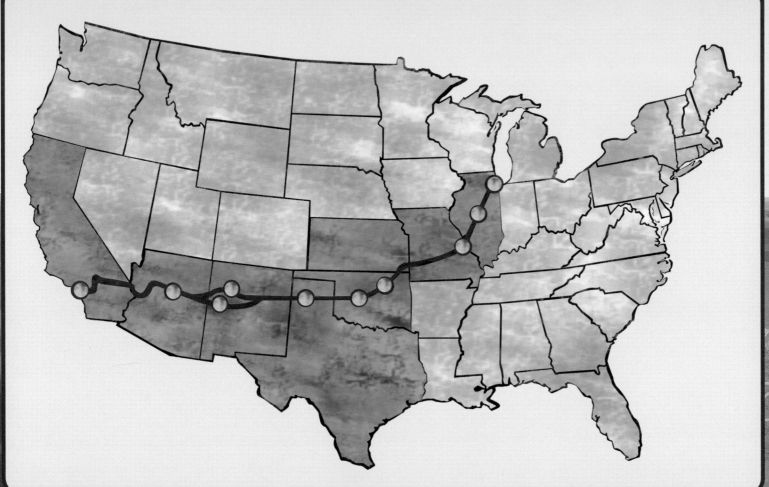

Sally is happy with McQueen's road paving. She invites him to stay at her motel.

The next day, McQueen goes into Doc Hudson's garage — and discovers that years ago, Doc won three Piston Cups! Doc refuses to discuss it.

Then Sally takes McQueen for a drive outside of town. She explains that Radiator Springs used to be a stopping place for tourists until the Interstate was built.

"The town got bypassed just to save ten minutes of driving," Sally says.

Back in town at Doc's garage, McQueen asks Doc about his racing career. Doc says that the racing world forgot about him after his big wreck in '54.

"They moved right on to the next rookie," Doc says. "But these are good folks around here, who care about one another. When was the last time you cared about something except yourself?"

McQueen can't come up with an answer. He stays up all night to finish paving the road.  The next day, while Sally and the others admire McQueen's work, reporters from all over the country come to town!

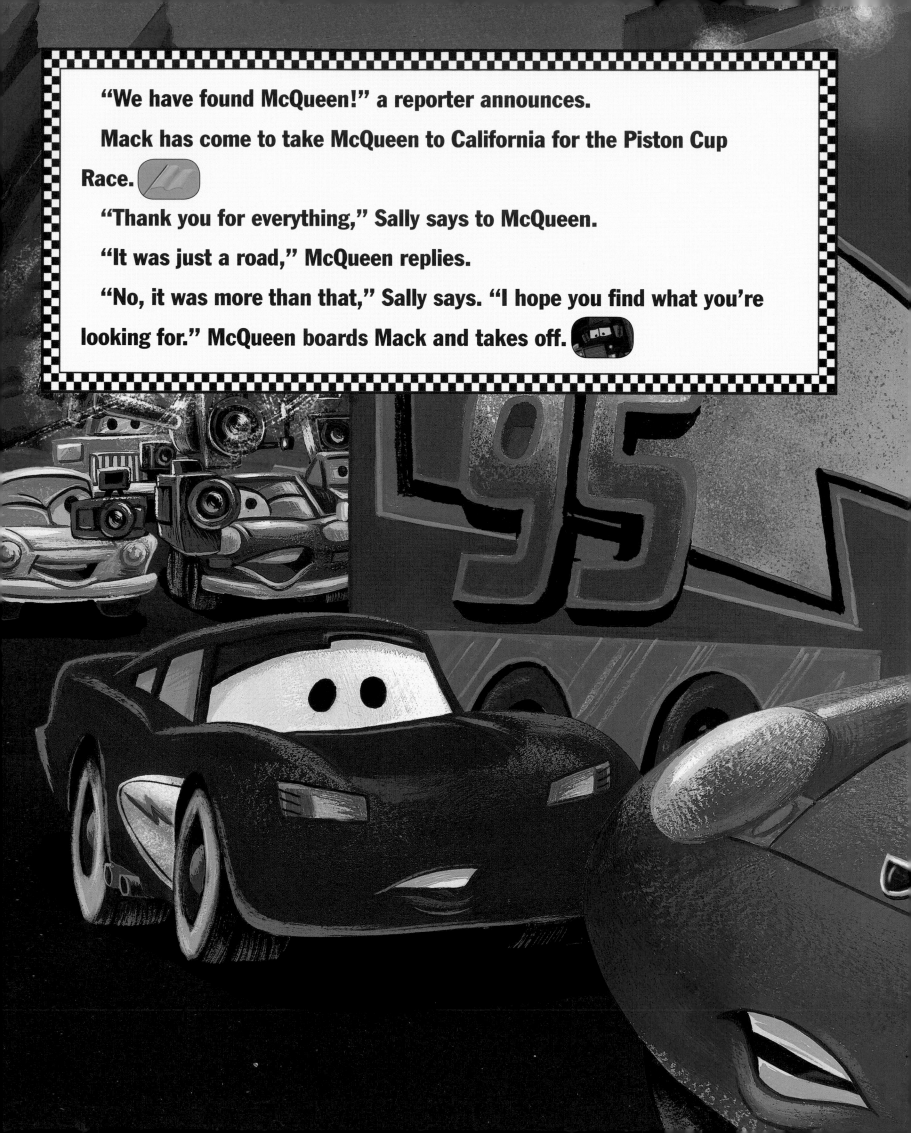

"We have found McQueen!" a reporter announces.

Mack has come to take McQueen to California for the Piston Cup Race.

"Thank you for everything," Sally says to McQueen.

"It was just a road," McQueen replies.

"No, it was more than that," Sally says. "I hope you find what you're looking for." McQueen boards Mack and takes off.

At last, the Piston Cup tie-breaker race is underway!  But McQueen trails behind Chick and The King. He can't stop thinking about his new friends back in Radiator Springs. Suddenly he hears a voice on his radio: "If you can drive as good as you can fix a road, then you can win."

It's Doc! He has come with some of the Radiator Springs gang to be McQueen's pit crew!

With encouragement from his friends, McQueen zooms past Chick and The King!  One of McQueen's tires blows out. But a speedy fix by his new pit crew keeps him in the lead.

Then, on the last lap, Chick angrily rams into The King. McQueen, just inches from the finish line, slams on his brakes and zips back to help. Chick takes first place. Then McQueen pushes The King over the finish line.

Race to
the
Finish!

Though Chick won the race, the crowd thinks McQueen is the real winner!  A big company offers to be McQueen's new sponsor. McQueen turns them down, but asks for one favor – a helicopter ride for his friend.

Back in Radiator Springs, Mater happily swoops through the sky.  Down below, McQueen tells Sally that he has returned to Radiator Springs for good to set up his racing headquarters.

"Oh well, there goes the town," Sally smiles.

5 6 7 8 10 12 14 16

AM FM ◄ ►

1 2 3 4 5

1. Down in the Valley

Down in the valley,
The valley so low,
Hang your head over,
Hear the wind blow.

2. Shenandoah

Oh Shenandoah, I long to hear you,
Away, you rolling river,
Oh Shenandoah, I long to hear you,
Away, I'm bound away,
'Cross the wide Missouri.

3. Home on the Range

Home, home on the range,
Where the deer and the antelope play,
Where seldom is heard a discouraging word,
And the skies are not cloudy all day.

4. There's a Long, Long Trail

There's a long, long trail a-winding
To the land where dreams come true,
And one day I'll be going down
That long, long trail with you.

5. We'll Be Comin' Round the Mountain

We'll be comin' round the mountain when we come.
We'll be comin' round the mountain when we come.
We'll be comin' round the mountain,
We'll be comin' round the mountain,
We'll be comin' round the mountain when we come.

You tell the story!

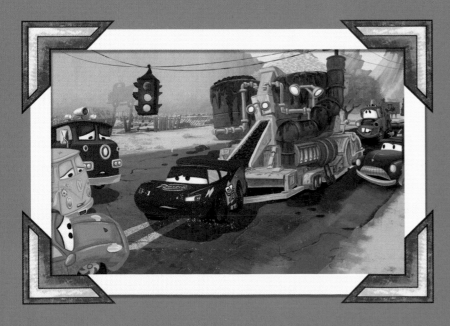